Snow Falls

Kate Gardner

ILLUSTRATED BY
Brandon James Scott

tundra

Snow
starts.

Snow

softens.

Snow tricks.

Snow tracks.

Snow
blows.

Snow
glows.

Snow

slides.

Snow
hides.

Snow

snows . . .

and snows . . .

and snows.

Snow

smiles.

Snow shields.

**Snow
flies.**

Snow
glides . . .

Until, at last — snow
goes!

For Froy, who loves snow
— K.G.

For Perley James and Betts
— B.J.S.

Tundra Books, an imprint of Penguin Random House Canada Young Readers, a division of Penguin Random House of Canada Limited

Library and Archives Canada Cataloguing in Publication

Title: Snow falls / Kate Gardner ; illustrated by Brandon James Scott.
Names: Gardner, Kate (Children's author), author. | Scott, Brandon James, 1982- illustrator.
Identifiers: Canadiana (print) 20190127880 | Canadiana (ebook) 20190127899 | ISBN 9781101919217 (hardcover) | ISBN 9781101919224 (EPUB) | ISBN 9780735271869 (special markets)
Subjects: LCSH: Snow—Juvenile literature. | LCSH: Winter—Juvenile literature.
Classification: LCC QC926.37 .G37 2020 | DDC j551.57/84—dc23

Published simultaneously in the United States of America by Tundra Books of Northern New York, an imprint of Penguin Random House Canada Young Readers, a division of Penguin Random House of Canada Limited

Library of Congress Control Number: 2019943029

Edited by Tara Walker with assistance from Margot Blankier
Designed by John Martz
The artwork in this book was painted digitally in the evenings of a snowy Canadian winter.
The text was set in Futura Bold.

Printed in China

www.penguinrandomhouse.ca

3   4   5   25   24   23

tundra

Penguin
Random House
TUNDRA BOOKS